DOUBLE TEAMING THE MAID

DIRTY BILLIONAIRE BOSS

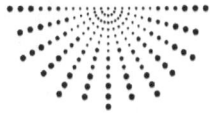

TALA MELTON

plicit Press
Erotica Fiction

GET NAUGHTY UPDATES

Click here or Visit
TalaMelton.com
for more Naughty Maid Stories

Double Teaming The Maid: Dirty Billionaire Boss

Digital Edition 1 is Copyright © 2020 by Tala Melton. All rights reserved.

eISBN: 978-1-62327-708-6

Print ISBN: 978-1-62327-709-3

CHAPTER ONE

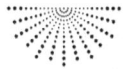

"*S*o, here we are..." Alex said, stating the obvious.

"Yes, Alex, we know!" Trey Alexander, an *old money billionaire,* was already irritated that the Aspen weather was acting up. The phrase 'act of god' never settled well with him because, well, he thought he was *God.*

Amy watched these two men who fought billionaire battles on the daily be reduced to two little boys who can't go and play outside because it's raining. Or, in this case, snowing.

She poured each of them a drink, a *play nicely* gesture, which worked. Both men settled in front of the fire and just appreciated that they were not caught in this weather. There was really nothing that they could do.

"I'll get started on dinner," Amy said.

"Leave it, not yet. Pour yourself a drink, sit... You're not here as *just* my maid..." Something about the way Trey called her a *maid* was reassuring. It really was just one of her jobs with Mr. Alexander, and there really was nothing wrong with calling the job by what it was.

Amy poured herself a drink and settled on the sofa next

to Alex. Trey occupied the armchair opposite, closest to the fire. It *was* a bit early to start with dinner and, even if the chef who had been hired for the weekend had made it to the cabin, he would probably not have started dinner for at least another hour or two.

"So, tell us a bit about yourself..." Alex asked, looking at Amy over the top of his glass.

"This isn't an interview, Alex... And must you start every sentence with *so?*" Trey's irritation was creeping back.

Amy took a sip from her own drink and just watched this exchange. It was rather entertaining, although she wasn't sure what she would do if it escalated. Two trapped bulls were no fun, no matter the day of the week. She took Alex's glass from him, then Trey's, and refilled both.

"I don't mind, Mr. Alexander," she said, handing them the drinks. She sat down in her seat, next to Alex, and narrated a short, relevant history for his benefit. Trey already knew everything that Alex was just hearing for the first time.

"The classic small-town girl with big city dreams, huh," Alex asked.

"I guess..." Amy said, looking at Trey while Alex's eyes were still firmly fixed on her.

"*So*..." Alex started.

"Shut up, Alex!" Trey said, the sternness in his voice making Amy look at him. He was smiling, so she wasn't sure what this meant. She hadn't worked close enough with him to know his little nuances.

"It's really fine," Amy said, looking Alex square in his eyes now, ready for whatever probing question he was about to ask.

"Do you have a boyfriend," he asked.

"No, do you," she responded.

Trey laughed out loud. He looked from Amy to Alex and back to Amy. He was really amused, not having realized before just how quick and clever Amy was. She'd been working for him for a few months only, and she handled all the various responsibilities well. But she had always just done her job, not really engaging with him beyond this.

"Yes, Alex... Do you have a *boyfriend?*" Trey asked.

Alex shrugged it off, not bothered. He was always easy about laughing at himself, and he had the ability to see the humor in most things. He moved closer to Amy now and put his face practically in hers before saying, "No... No, boyfriend!"

They all laughed now. Amy poured them all one more drink, sat down, and enjoyed it, chatting easily with her boss and his business partner. When she was done, she got up and did get dinner started. Not sure what would be dinner; she just took food out of the fridge and cupboard, waiting to be inspired.

"She's very pretty..." Alex said to Trey.

"I thought you liked blondes?" Trey asked.

"I wasn't talking about her hair..."

Amy put dinner together, a salad, and grilled chicken breasts. She got two bottles of wine from the cellar, and they, all three, sat down to eat. They still chatted easily. It was comfortable now and relaxed, and even the banter between Trey and Alex was increasingly humorous, playful even.

"So..." Alex started.

"So?" Trey and Amy asked together.

"Do you have a type?" Alex was looking at Amy now.

CHAPTER TWO

*A*fter dinner, and a rather lengthy conversation about Amy not having a particular type, they sat close to the fire again, cognac in hand to warm them from the inside, the fire doing an excellent job of the outside. Alex was looking at Amy like he wanted to eat her up like she was food, and Amy kept looking at Trey to see if he'd noticed.

"She's not a steak," Trey said to Alex suddenly.

Amy laughed out loud, not expecting this comment from her boss.

"She does look particularly edible though, don't you think," he asked Alex, looking at Amy.

She blushed!

"Well, I don't think she'd want to be eaten by you!"

Amy looked from Trey to Alex. She settled her gaze on Alex for a while, noticing him for the first time. It was actually the first time she looked at him like a man. He was what, 45, she thought, and he really wasn't bad looking. She knew he worked out every day, just because Trey was his workout partner, his *gym buddy*, and had been for as long as she'd worked for him, and for years prior.

He was greying; Trey was too. And while they looked very different, they were both good looking. In fact, calling them *handsome* was a bit of an understatement. Her eyes went from Alex to Trey, who she had also never quite looked at as anything but her boss before this minute.

"Why not," Amy asked, suddenly, and both men looked at her now. She sipped the warm brown liquid from her glass, her eyes on the flames, feeling their penetrative gaze. She wondered if she wasn't starting down a path she might not be able to get off, but now, it was too late.

"Yes, Trey, why not?"

"Well, she may as well be eaten by me in that case, and I don't see a 23-year old playing with two old *geysers* like us!" Trey was also taking this conversation down a path from which there really was no return so that they were all suddenly nervous that it might get awkward.

The was a moment, a long, drawn-out moment, where they all just focused on their drinks. Everybody was searching for an appropriate '*get out*' clause, a suitable escape phrase, but nothing. Trey was looking at Amy again, who was looking at the flames. Alex was watching Trey, trying to get his attention, trying to say something with his eyes that even if Trey looked at him, he wouldn't understand.

"Another one, before I call it a night," Amy said at last. She thought it best to remove herself from the equation, just to give them the freedom to discuss her at leisure. From the way Alex was looking at her, he clearly had a lot on his mind.

"I'll take one," Alex said.

"Why not," Trey added.

When she got up to pour the drinks, Alex and Trey looked at each other now. Alex mouthed, "Do you think she'd be open to it."

Trey mouthed, "No!"

Alex started to say, "Ask her," when Amy suddenly

returned with the drinks. She sat down closer to Alex now, making the middle-aged man more than a little uncomfortable. He was growing a massive bulge in his pants that he couldn't hide.

"So, what were we talking about?" Alex asked, again looking at Trey, who was remembering the last time he and Alex had *shared a toy*.

It was a couple of months ago, on a business trip to Spain. They had talked two-holiday makers into going back to their respective hotel rooms. One of the women got a little too drunk and needed to sleep it off, the other willing to make up for her friend's poor behavior.

Alex and Trey were both the epitome of the Alpha male. They were aggressive, went after what they wanted, and were unapologetic about the things they wanted. The two of them in any sort of a *menage*, if Spain was anything to go by, was not the best idea. They were both extremely virile, with insatiable appetites, and more fetishes than should be normal for a single person. While the threesome in Madrid was fun, it left the woman whose name none of them could remember, tired and tender. She'd refused to speak to them the next day, in fact, saying that she would take a year to recover, but she did thank them.

She'd also said they'd put many men half their age to shame.

This was months ago, though, and while both of them remembered this quite differently, there was something about it that appealed to both of them. Actually, Amy appealed to both of them now, and they knew that forcing her to choose between them would be unfair, only because there was no chance of getting anybody else up to the cabin right now to make it two for two.

Trey told himself over and over again that he was going to bed after this drink. Alex was still trying for a way to get the three of them to play, but nothing was coming to mind. He knew that Trey knew Amy better and that he seemed uninterested was starting to irritate him. Amy was playing with the idea, but only just. The banter between them had been playful and pleasant, but that's really all it was.

Sleeping with her boss was never on her radar, and despite the weather, despite the fact that they were stuck in a beautiful cabin in Aspen, despite the fact that they were all attractive, all sexual, even sleeping with her boss's business partner seemed too much of a faux pas to make, despite the circumstances.

And the circumstance really lent itself to what they were and were not suggesting. The banter had been more than a little suggestive, more than a little leading, but the three of them, despite looking in the same general direction, they failed to land on the same page. Alex was the most frustrated.

"How long have you two been friends," Amy asked, an attempt to change the subject.

"35 years," Trey answered.

"And who's the most competitive?"

"We both are, that's why we decided to go into business together..." Trey and Amy seemed to be having a sensible, subdued conversation now.

"We might be equally competitive, but I'm definitely better at most things," Alex said.

"Like what?" Trey asked.

"Most things," Alex said, bring his fave close to Amy's as he whispered this response. Again, Amy blushed.

Everything Alex said was loaded. And Amy found herself curious now, wanting to see what they might do if they had to compete to please her...

CHAPTER THREE

"*M*aybe we should set up a challenge; we've got the time, after all!" Amy was leading now.

"What kind of challenge," Alex asked.

"I don't know, a kissing competition," Trey said, surprising everyone with this juvenile suggestion. He thought that Amy would object, though, so he felt comfortable making this suggestion.

"Okay, who's first?" Amy asked, also surprising everyone.

Trey ushered Alex, doing the gentlemanly thing, letting the competition go first. Alex was closest to Amy anyway, so it just made sense. Alex downed his drink and looked at Amy, needing her to put her glass down.

When she did, he put a hand behind her head and pulled her towards him. His full lips were hot on hers, his tongue moving into her mouth in a way that said he knew exactly what he was doing. She found herself kissing him back almost immediately.

They kissed much longer than they expected, Trey watching them closely, himself suddenly aroused. Alex couldn't hide his bulge now if he tried, and he wasn't sure what she would do when she saw this. He held her face so that he could control the direction of her eyes. But there was nothing he could do about preventing her from seeing, Amy looking flushed, embarrassed for him.

"Sorry," Alex said.

"I think it's best if you came over here," Trey said. "He might have a little trouble moving!"

Amy came to Trey, who motioned for her to sit on his lap. She did, again, comfortable with the playfulness. This really was all just a big joke, she felt, Trey, feeling the same. They were just passing the time, just messing around.

Trey kissed her with the determined passion of an old lover. He had one eye on her thigh, the other on her neck. He wasn't pulling her to him, just holding her in place. Her thigh rubbed against where he was also hard now, and there was nothing he could do about it. Trey had the kind of cock that he couldn't hide flaccid. Hard, it was impossible!

"So, who won," Trey asked when he pulled his mouth from her, Amy still on his lap. She looked over to where Alex was struggling to position himself in his pants in a way that was comfortable. He was not succeeding.

"I'm not sure," she said. She really wasn't. They both kissed very very nicely. In fact, both kisses were incredible, similar, and different at the same time—both of them arousing her just a little.

She undid the top button of her shirt, suddenly feeling very hot. Alex was also unbuttoning his own shirt, though what he really wanted to be doing was undoing the button on his trousers. Still, on Trey's lap, she swung around and looked at Alex. He stood up and walked towards her, bending down, kissing her long again. Both men were incredibly aroused now, and while Amy's own arousal wasn't as instant, it was certainly making an appearance.

When she pulled her mouth from Alex, she turned to

Trey again, and she was kissing him now. She kissed him long, and she kissed him deeply. She was still comparing them to each other for a moment, and then suddenly, she wasn't. Suddenly she was just kissing Trey and then Alex, Alex and then Trey, just because she really, really wanted to.

"Nope, I can't do it... I can't decide," she said.

"Maybe this will help you decide," Alex said, and he took his shirt off. Alex stood up, effectively removing Amy from his lap. He sat her down in the armchair now, and he too removed his shirt. He looked at Alex as he took his boots off, and Alex, taking his cue, kicked off his shoes and took his trousers off quickly. They were both now down to their underwear.

Amy put her hands in front of her eyes. She parted her fingers so she could see, and then brought the fingers together again so that her eyes were once again blocked. She was red now, not embarrassment, *something else!*

They looked at each other, consensus, and took Amy by the hands, brought her off the chair so that she was standing between them. They *helped* her out of her shirt, almost disappointed that she had a tank top underneath it. Alex worked on her jeans quickly. He needed to get the pieces of denim off her before they stopped *playing* this game.

Amy laughed very loudly throughout. She laughed when Trey took off her shoes, laughed louder when her jeans made their way down her legs. It really was *playtime, bordering dangerously on fun time!*

All three of them were in their underwear now, and again nobody knew how to proceed. Maybe they knew how, but nobody was sure *how!* Trey went to pour them all another drink, knowing that alcohol always helped. He was also so hard now that he hoped that leaving Alex alone with Amy, the two of them would start the next progression of the

"When in doubt, drink!" he said, handing the drinks to the two he found kissing again. It was clear that they were going to do whatever they decided to do, and Trey just hoped that they all decided on the same thing.

"Are you going to take that off," Alex asked, pointing to her tank top. She pulled it off in one effortless movement, revealing the most beautiful bra either man had ever seen in their lives.

They sat on the rug, drank. They chatted for a while before Alex pulled Amy down to lying. She was on her back, looking every bit like *Miss December.* Both men lay down on either side of her. They both ran a single finger up and down the length of her body. If it's a competition she wanted, then a competition she would get. Amy was not ready for what was about to happen to her.

Or maybe she was because her hands found both men's bulges, still hidden by underwear. She moved her fingers up and down the thick curves, both men having a bend that differed only in degrees. Amy thought, to herself, that this similarity was uncanny. Similar cocks were really a strange reason to be friends, but here they were.

Trey took his underwear off first, and while Alex got his own off, Trey was pulling Amy's panties down. He was suddenly the more eager of the two.

Amy came up just so that Alex could remove her bra, and they all brought their glasses together. They sipped their drinks, put them down, and Amy once more took her place between them, reclining like a *centerfold.*

Alex kissed her mouth again. He was kissing her with a passion that belied the nature of their relationship. Alex was sucking on her nipples, enjoying both of them in equal amounts for a while before he had to give one up to Trey.

They both seemed to have decided that Amy would be

treated with the utmost care because she really didn't have to be doing this, but here she was, naked, offering herself to them, for what she hoped would be a mutual pleasure.

CHAPTER FOUR

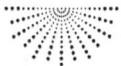

*T*heir movements were incredibly synchronized. It was as though they had rehearsed the way they both were touching her lower lips with just their index finger. They tapped it, gently, tap tap tap. Then they were tracing similar patterns on just the outside of her. Their fingers dance with each other and passed each other, bringing every part of her that mattered between her thighs to a wonderful life. And they never skipped a single beat with their mouths on her nipples.

"So..." Alex started.

"Not now, Alex," Trey said, bringing his mouth to hers again, kissing her full on her mouth. Alex gave up the sentence he was about to say, the question he was about to ask, in favor of tracing a clear path with his own mouth to her other lips. He positioned himself between her legs and proceeded to French kiss her there while Trey French kissed her mouth. Both men were experts at what they were doing, and if she had to choose, if she was pressed to make a decision, then Trey would definitely have won the kissing competition.

Then Trey's mouth was off hers. He, too, traced a path down to the beautiful place where her legs met, the place her thighs opened up into ecstasy. He wanted to explore this place, this not so secret place that she was offering up willingly. Alex let him join him down there, and with just their tongues, they delivered ecstasy after erotic ecstasy into Amy that she started to flow.

She was bordering on climax but not quite. When one man's mouth brought her close, the other one took her back. They worked in perfect synchronicity, giving her suspended orgasm after suspended orgasm so that her legs shook. She needed to cum now. Every part of her needed the orgasm that seemed just out of reach. Alex and Trey looked at each other, Alex conceding this time, allowing her boss the privilege of getting her over the first time.

He got up and went to see what other drinks the bar had. It really was fully stocked so that finding a bottle of tequila was easy. He went to the kitchen to get what he needed to prepare classic tequila shots while Trey put Amy out of her misery, with just his mouth.

As good as Trey had been on her mouth, he was an expert on her lower lips. He licked the outside of her until again she was quivering. Then his tongue was inside her, and he was frenching her vagina. He moved his tongue inside her until she was expelling more hot, sticky liquid than either of them had thought was humanly possible.

She really came hard, and Alex watched her shudder, he watched her shake. He watched as Trey held her down gently and brought her to an epic end before easing her off the cliff he had just thrown her from. She couldn't speak; it was her turn to be embarrassed. Amy was a squirter, something which excited both men, so much so that they both had to mention it.

The men had the first shots while Amy recovered. Then

she joined them, and they had several shots. With no meet-
ings, nowhere to be, this was perfectly acceptable. It was also
so that, if all else failed and tomorrow there were any regrets,
they had the option of blaming it on the alcohol...

Amy was still wet when Alex put a single finger inside
her. He fingered her with just this one finger for a while
before turning her over onto her stomach. He parted her legs
and went inside her again with just his middle finger, playing
with her asshole with his thumb. He used her own juices to
lubricate her hole, and then again, he was middle finger deep
inside her, his thumb settled quite completely in her other
hole.

It was Trey who watched for a while until he couldn't. He
lay down next to her so that she could reach his throbbing
erection with her mouth. As soon as her lips wrapped
around him, he breathed a sigh of relief. He hadn't realized
that he was desperate now to be touched there, that he
needed to be satisfied, so close was he to imploding. He
reclined, leaning backwards so that she could work on him,
while Alex prepared both her holes.

When Alex's fingers were out of her, she was left wanting.
Not for long, though, because Alex came upon her and sent
himself completely into her front from the back. There were
no rules, nobody calling dibs on any part of her. He thrust
into her in slow, languid thrusts savoring each stroke. He had
no plan to orgasm, not yet, but he too just needed some sort
of relief before she had another orgasm.

Amy was in heaven, though, having a second epic climax.
Alex was nowhere near his own end, but this had no bearing
on Amy's responses to having him inside her. He drove
himself into her over and over again until she was done, Trey
thrusting deeper into her mouth now, opened wider because
she was exhaling hard.

Trey held her head in place; he was suddenly close. He

held her mouth on him until he was expelling his seed into her mouth. He pushed her down hard on himself, hands on her head until he too was done. There seemed to be a collective sigh of relief between the two of them, Alex taking it easy.

Alex pulled himself from her front, and with her still on her stomach, using just her own juices as lube again, he went into her asshole with one swift stroke. He went in easy despite the tightness, because Amy was, unbeknown to them, an anal goddess. She loves taking it there.

It was his turn to orgasm now, so he lay himself on top of her and thrust, short quick thrusts, rapid movements of his pelvis feeding her over and over again with the full length of himself. His arms went under hers, her mouth still on Trey, as over and over again, he fed himself into her. He still had no urgency, but it just seemed fair that he too should have an orgasm. When it happened, after many, many strokes, it was very, very loud, so that they all *laughed out loud.*

It seemed that laughter would be a present part of tonight's festivities. They all had another shot before Amy was again on her back. She lifted her legs and touched herself, moved her own hands over her own breasts, and then fingering the lips that were quickly wanting attention again. She hadn't thought they would be so decent about it, so civil. The way they had spoken about their competitive nature, Amy really expected that these two would try to one-up each other. Instead, here they were playing very, very nice.

She sent a finger into herself hard. She added another finger and moved them hard inside herself. She was showing them how she wanted to be taken now, not sure who would be up to the challenge. Alex watched her smiled. Trey downed another shot of tequila for courage, and he got down on the floor on top of her.

CHAPTER FIVE

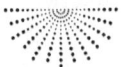

*H*e wasn't as hard as he needed to be, but he knew it wouldn't be very long. He rubbed himself against the outside of her, easy, gentle, bringing himself to life again. As soon as he was at full mast again, he went into her, all the way. Amy gasped, so completely was the way Trey took her. He watched her face as he fed his thick self into her repeatedly. Trey was firing hard, and he was firing fast. If she wanted it rough, then rough is what she would get.

"Take it like you mean it," Alex said, again bring the room to laughter. Trey wasn't laughing though, taking what he was doing very, very seriously. He put his hands underneath her, grabbed her ass, pushed her up into him as he pushed himself down and into her. His strokes were complete. His entry was full, as was his exit. Trey shot himself all the way into her and then pulled himself all the way out. He did this over and over without looking down for direction. He knew exactly where he was going.

He turned them onto their sides and went in harder. Over and over again, he gave her everything he had. All of him was inside her for the longest time. Then he was out of her completely.

Trey turned her so that she faced away from him, went into her completely again. He could see himself moving inside her now, and this made him harder. So he went deeper. Every time she thought he couldn't possibly grow anymore, he did. Trey penis had taken on a life of its own now, and this life had nothing to do with him anymore. He seemed to have lost all control of the appendage.

He went in so deep that Amy couldn't breathe now. It was okay, though, who needed to breathe. He put an arm under her so that his hand was on her breasts. The other handheld her belly and held her in place, so that she couldn't move now even if she tried. He fed her all ten solid inches of himself so hard that she thought she might pass out. She didn't, though, needing to concentrate on Alex, who was not shoving his own cock in her mouth.

Both holes stuffed, she waited for her orgasm. She knew that it was a matter of time, Trey hitting her just how she needed to be hit if this was going to be possible. And it was possible. Amy came harder now than she had all night. She came so hard that she couldn't do anything with her mouth except open it. Alex moved himself in and out of her mouth, worked himself to his own end. By the time he shot his load into her open mouth, she was well and truly done.

Trey wasn't, though, needing one more orgasm. He was close, but her front was spent. He rolled her onto her stomach when he pulled from her and drove himself into the hole that saw Alex to his first orgasm. He delivered a dozen perfectly executed strokes until he was also done. The three of them lay in a heap on the floor; nobody was able to move for a minute. Then they gathered themselves just enough to get to their bedrooms, and into much-needed showers.

Amy decided on a bath. She lay in the hot water watching

the snow come down hard through her large window. It really was beautiful here, she thought, even at night. So this weekend didn't go according to plan, but now she knew, as did Alex and Trey, that at least the weekend wouldn't be a total waste.

ABOUT THE AUTHOR

Tala Melton is an emerging erotica author of naughty maids and their billionaire bosses.

Readers: I want to expand a few of the stories to see where the characters can be explored further. If there are any of the stories that you would like to read more about again, I'd love to hear from you!

Visit my blog at Tala Melton Blog
Join my newsletter for free exclusive previews Tala Melton Newsletter
Follow me on Twitter at Tala Melton Twitter
Like my page on Facebook at Tala Melton FB

Sign up for Free Stories from Xplicit Press Authors
Xplicit Press Updates
Like Xplicit Press on Facebook
Follow Xplicit Press on Twitter

MORE NAUGHTY MAID STORIES BY TALA MELTON

Naughty Maids and The Dirty Billionaire Bosses